CHANGES

Written by **Marjorie N. Allen** and **Shelley Rotner**

Photographs by **Shelley Rotner**

Aladdin Paperbacks

First Aladdin Paperbacks edition October 1995
Text copyright © 1991 by Marjorie N. Allen and Shelley Rotner
Illustrations copyright © 1991 by Shelley Rotner

Aladdin Paperbacks
An imprint of Simon & Schuster
Children's Publishing Division
1230 Avenue of the Americas
New York, NY 10020

Also available in a Macmillan Books for Young Readers edition

The text of this book was set in 20-point Jensen.
The photographs were taken on 35mm Kodachrome film
and reproduced from color transparencies.
Manufactured in Hong Kong

10 9 8 7 6 5 4 3 2 1

The Library of Congress has cataloged the hardcover edition as follows:
Allen, Marjorie N.
Changes / written by Marjorie N. Allen and Shelley Rotner ;
photographs by Shelley Rotner. — 1st ed.   p.   cm.
Summary: Describes, in rhymed text and illustrations, how things
in nature change as they grow and develop.
[1. Nature—Fiction. 2. Stories in rhyme.] I. Rotner, Shelley, ill.
II. Title.   PZ8.3.A4192Ch 1991   [E]—dc20 90-6601
ISBN 0-02-700252-7

ISBN 0-689-80068-1 (Aladdin pbk.)

For Dena with love
—M.N.A.

For Emily and Stephen,
the best changes in my life
—S.R.

All things go through changes

as they grow.

From fiddleheads to uncurled ferns,

scattered pinecones — forest tall;

flowers peek through one last snow

as winter's gray turns to green.

Milkweed clusters bloom in spring;

and feathered seeds in autumn
dance lightly in the wind.

Sun gives way to clouds,
clouds and wind to rain,

and winter's cold brings
ice and snow.

Seasons change —

leaves fall.

Spring blossoms yield summer fruit;

in autumn, corn grows high.

All things change,

then change again.

From fragile eggs

to birds

in flight,

from spotted fawn to great-horned buck,

and piglet small

to giant sow.

Horses, too — foal to mare.

All things

go through changes

as they grow.